D0574685

KITSAP REGIONAL LIBRARY
3 9068 00921 2616

DATE DUE

| NOV 0 9 1996 | MAY 1 8 2000 | |
| DEC 1 8 1996 | MAR 3 0 | |

JUV ROT
LB 1/02
N

BOOKMOBILE
MANCHESTER 8/00
KINGSTON 5/01
BREMERTON
LITTLE BOSTON

CROW AND HAWK

For Helen
Special thanks to Jackie Fortey and Alison Moss
for their help with this book
—J. C.

A B O U T   T H I S   S T O R Y

This tale was originally told by a well-known, elderly Native American storyteller of the Cochiti Pueblo near Santa Fe, New Mexico. In 1928 she shared this story in her native language, Keresan, with a story collector named Ruth Benedict. The story was included in a collection by Benedict titled *Tales of the Cochiti Indians,* which was published in 1931 by the University of New Mexico Press. When the publisher revised the collection in 1981, an introduction by Alfonso Ortiz was added. In that introduction, Ortiz says this story was of the kind that was once "learned by the fireside during long autumn and winter evenings as a normal part of growing up."

– Michael Rosen

First published in 1995 by Studio Editions Limited
Text copyright © 1995 by Michael Rosen
Illustrations copyright © 1995 by John Clementson

All rights reserved. No part of this publication may be reproduced or transmitted in any form or by any means,
electronic or mechanical, including photocopy, recording, or any information storage and
retrieval system, without permission in writing from the publisher.

Requests for permission to make copies of any part of the work should be mailed to: Permissions Department,
Harcourt Brace & Company, 6277 Sea Harbor Drive, Orlando, Florida 32887-6777.

First U.S. edition 1995
Library of Congress Cataloging-in-Publication Data is available upon request.

LC #94-15176   ISBN 0-15-200257-X
Printed in Singapore
A B C D E

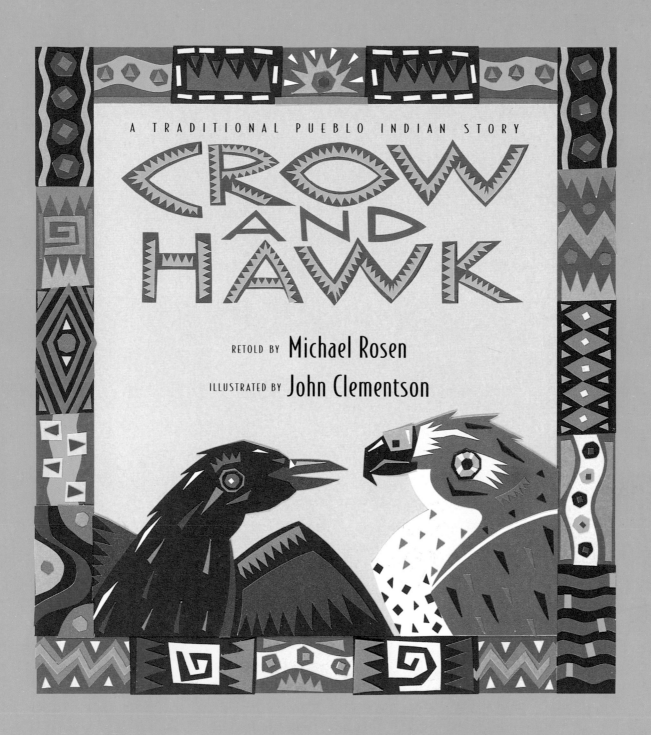

A TRADITIONAL PUEBLO INDIAN STORY

CROW AND HAWK

RETOLD BY **Michael Rosen**

ILLUSTRATED BY **John Clementson**

HARCOURT BRACE & COMPANY

SAN DIEGO NEW YORK LONDON

Crow had a nest with eggs in it.

She sat and sat and sat.
Nothing happened.

She sat and sat and sat.
Nothing happened.

Crow got tired of all this sitting and sitting, so she flew away.

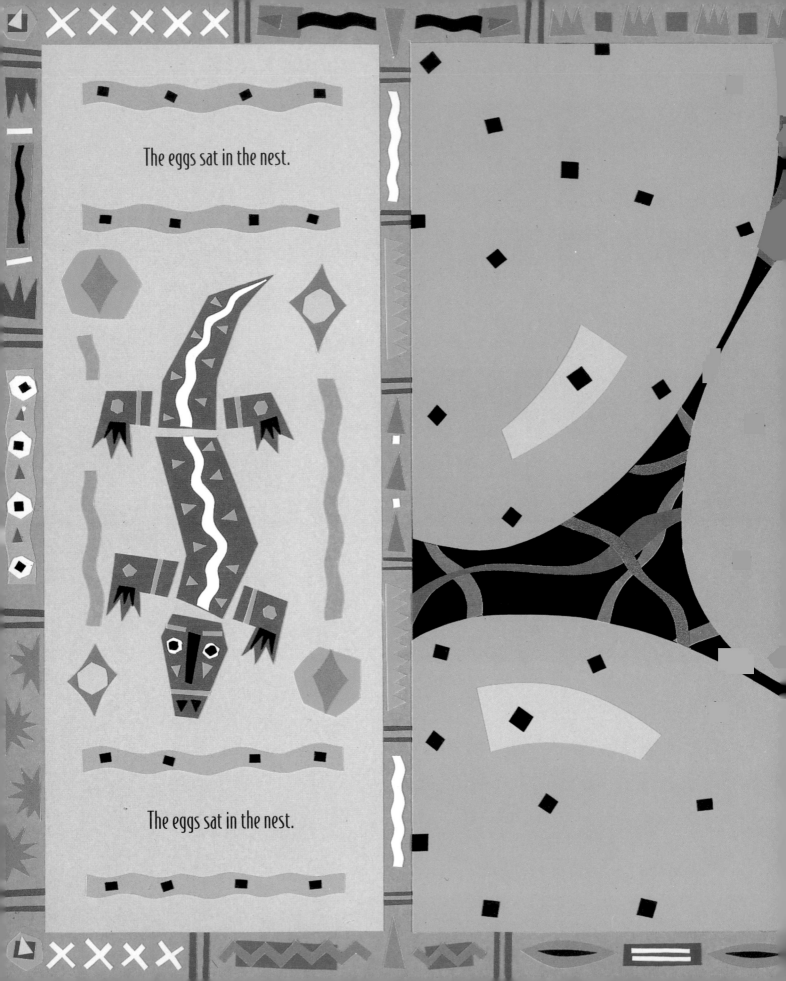

The eggs sat in the nest.

The eggs sat in the nest.

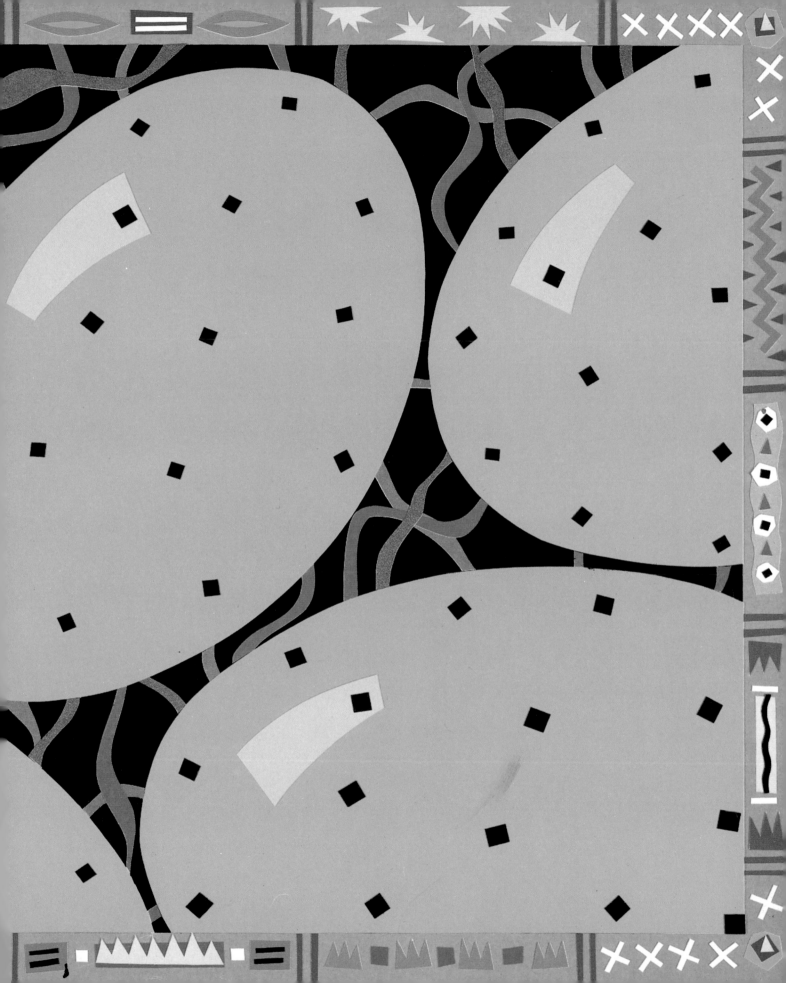

Soon, Hawk came by. Hawk said to herself,
"The bird who owns this nest
no longer cares for it. I will sit on these
poor little eggs."

Hawk sat on the eggs.
She sat and sat and sat.
Nobody came to the nest.

The eggs began to hatch, but no crow came.
The little crows crept out of their shells,
and Hawk flew about getting food for them.

The little crows got bigger and bigger, their
feathers grew, their wings got strong,
and Hawk fetched and carried for them
all day long.

Crow was out and about one day, when suddenly she remembered her nest and flew back to it.
There she found Hawk taking care of the little crows.

"Hawk!" screeched Crow.

"What do you want?" asked Hawk.

"Give me back those little crows!"

"Why?" asked Hawk.

"Because they're mine," said Crow.

Hawk fluffed up her feathers and said,
"You laid the eggs to be sure,
but then you went off and left them.
I came by and sat on the nest.
For many days, as I watched over the eggs,
I didn't eat a thing. Since they hatched I've
been working hard to keep them fed.
I'm not giving them back."

"Well, I'm taking them back!" said Crow.

"No, you aren't," said Hawk. "Where were you when I was looking after your children? You're too late. They're staying with me."

"Very well," said Crow, "I shall take this matter to the King of the Birds and see what *he* has to say."

"Fine," agreed Hawk. "Let's go."
So Crow and Hawk went to see
Eagle, the King of the Birds.

"Why did you leave your nest?"
Eagle asked Crow. Crow said nothing.
"How did you come to find this nest?"
Eagle asked Hawk.
"I found a nest full of eggs with no one
sitting on it. I waited,
but no one came," said Hawk.
"But they are my children. I laid
the eggs," said Crow.
"As I was saying," said Hawk,
it was I who sat on the eggs.
I hatched them and fed the little ones.
I won't give them back."

Eagle spoke: "If you, Crow, really
cared for your young ones,
you wouldn't have left the nest.
Hawk has been their mother."
Crow said, "King, ask the little ones which
mother they want. Ask the little ones."
"Well?" Eagle asked the little crows.

"Hawk is the only mother we know,"
they replied.
"No, I am your real mother," protested Crow.
"Oh, no," said the little ones.
"Hawk hatched us. Hawk fed us. You left us."

So that's how it was settled. The little crows stayed with Hawk. Crow began to weep. "Don't cry," said Eagle, "this is the way it must be. You left the nest; you have lost the children."

And off went all the little crows with Hawk.